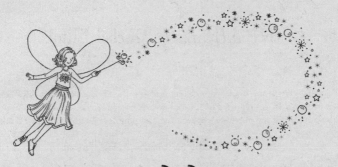

Gabby
the Bubble Gum
Fairy

To Tianna, who loves the fairies

Special thanks to Rachel Elliot

First published in the United Kingdom in 2017 by Orchard U.K., Carmelite House, 50 Victoria Embankment, London EC4Y 0DZ.

The publisher does not have any control over and does not assume any responsibility for author or third-party websites or their content.

This book is a work of fiction. Names, characters, places, and incidents are either the product of the author's imagination or are used fictitiously, and any resemblance to actual persons, living or dead, business establishments, events, or locales is entirely coincidental.

ISBN 978-1-338-20721-7

10 9 8 7 6 5 4 3   18 19 20 21 22

Printed in the U.S.A.   40
First printing 2018

Gabby
the Bubble Gum
Fairy

by Daisy Meadows

SCHOLASTIC INC.

Candy Factory

The Fairyland
Palace

Candy Factory
Orchard

Candy Land

Wetherbu

Park

The
Tree House
Club

Jack Frost's Ice Castle

Animal Shelter

Community Center

Children's Hospital

Give me candy! Give me sweets!
Give me sticky, chewy treats!
Lollipops and fudge so yummy—
Bring them here to fill my tummy.

Monica, I'll steal from you.
Gabby, Franny, Shelley, too.
I will build a candy shop,
So I can eat until I pop!

Contents

The Playground Buddy

Rachel Walker slid down the candy-cane slide. She squealed with laughter as she zoomed off the end onto a trampoline and bounced into the air.

"This is the best park in the whole wide world," she called happily to her best friend, Kirsty Tate, who was sitting at the top of the slide.

"WHEEEEEE!" Kirsty sang out as she shot down the slide and bounced down beside Rachel. "It's so much fun. I'm so glad that Aunt Helen asked us both to meet her here."

Rachel was staying with Kirsty for a whole week. It was always fun visiting Wetherbury, but this time it was extra exciting. Kirsty's aunt Helen, who worked at Candy Land, a candy factory, had asked the girls to help her with some very special deliveries. Candy Land was giving out Helping Hands awards for people who were doing wonderful things to help the community. It was part of Aunt Helen's job to present the winners with bags of their favorite candy, and Rachel and Kirsty were proud to help.

"Your aunt Helen should be here soon," said Rachel, checking her watch.

The girls stopped bouncing and looked over at the factory. The candy-themed park was on the beautiful grounds of the factory, on the outskirts of Wetherbury.

The tall slide looked as if it had been made from candy canes, the swings were shaped like jelly beans, and the merry-go-round looked like a big cookie. On the far side of the park, some boys were playing by a fence that seemed to be made of strawberry licorice laces.

Just then, Kirsty noticed a little boy
sitting on one end of the seesaw, which
was shaped like a hard candy stick.

"That little boy looks
sad," she said.
"I wonder if
he is lonely.
Maybe one of
us should go
sit on the
other end of
the seesaw so
he can actually
play on it."

"I think someone
else has the same idea,"
said Rachel.

A girl with long brown hair was
walking toward the seesaw, smiling. She

said something to the little boy, and a smile lit up his face. Then she sat on the other end of the seesaw and started to go up and down.

"What a kind thing to do," said Kirsty. "I noticed that girl earlier, pushing a little girl on the swings."

When the little boy's mom called him away, the girl left the seesaw and walked toward Rachel and Kirsty.

"Hi," she said in a friendly voice. "I haven't seen you here before. I'm Olivia. I'm the playground buddy for this park."

"I'm Rachel and

this is Kirsty," said Rachel. "I've never heard of a playground buddy before."

"I look out for anyone who seems lonely or on their own, and I make sure they have someone to play with," Olivia explained. "Sometimes people make new friends here. It's so great."

"What a nice idea," said Rachel with a smile. "What made you think of it?"

"When I moved to Wetherbury, I missed my old school and my old friends," said Olivia. "I remember how it felt to be lonely and have no one to play with. I want to make sure that no one else feels like that. So I play with children who are alone, and I help them meet new friends."

"It sounds as if you're not lonely anymore, either," said Kirsty.

"Definitely not," Olivia said, laughing.

"I always have friends to play with now that I'm a playground buddy."

"Every park should have one," said Rachel with a smile. "It's an idea I'll remember."

"Unfortunately, it doesn't seem to be

working very well with everyone today, though," said Olivia, glancing toward the strawberry–licorice lace fence. There were three boys huddled by it, looking around and laughing. "Those boys over there have driven most of the children away."

Surprise Under the Slide

The boys were all wearing matching hats, and they were blowing enormous green bubbles with bubble gum.

"What have they been doing?" asked Kirsty.

"They've said mean things to all the children, and they've been sticking their bubble gum everywhere and leaving a mess," Olivia explained. "No one wants to sit on a swing that's covered in chewed bubble gum."

She reached into her pocket and pulled out a pack of bubble gum.

"Would you like some?" she said. "I love bubble gum, but I always put it in the trash when I'm finished chewing. It makes me feel sad to see those boys spoil the playground for everyone else. They're being so rude."

Thanking her, Rachel and Kirsty each took a piece of the bright-pink bubble gum. Rachel popped hers in her mouth, but it was so hard that she couldn't chew it. She could see that Kirsty and Olivia were having the same problem. They took the gum out and dropped it into the nearby trash can.

"What happened to it?" asked Olivia in a disappointed voice. "I had a piece earlier and it was fine."

Just then, the gate to the playground squeaked, and a little girl came in.

"I'll go see if she wants someone to play with," said Olivia. "It was nice to meet you both, Rachel and Kirsty. See you later."

She walked toward the little girl, and Rachel turned to Kirsty.

"Want to go down the slide again?" she asked. "Oh!"

The space underneath the slide was glowing with a pink light, and both Rachel and Kirsty knew exactly what that meant. Magic! They had shared enough adventures with their fairy friends to know when another adventure was about to start.

The girls ducked under the slide and smiled. Gabby the Bubble Gum Fairy was fluttering in the shadow of the slide. She floated down and hovered in front of them. Her pink hair bounced on her shoulders, and her peach-colored skirt fluttered in the light breeze.

"Hello, Rachel and Kirsty," she said in a sweet voice. "I'm glad I found you. Will you help me get my magical bubble gum back from Jack Frost and his goblins?"

"Of course we will," said Kirsty at once. "We had so much fun helping Monica yesterday."

"She told me how wonderful you were," said Gabby. "I'm sure I can get my magical bubble gum back if I have

your help. I need it to make sure that all bubble gum is chewy and bubblicious."

The day before, Monica the Marshmallow Fairy had whisked Rachel and Kirsty to the Candy Factory, a special place in Fairyland where candy grew on trees. The Sweet Fairies—and their friends, the Sugar and Spice Fairies—were getting ready for the annual Candy Harvest. The trees were full of all kinds of delicious treats. But as the fairies were telling the girls about the Fairyland Harvest Feast, Jack Frost and his mischievous goblins had appeared. Before anyone could stop them, they had stolen the magical treats that belonged to the Sweet Fairies.

"We'll do everything we can to find your magical object," said Rachel. "We just tried some bubble gum, and it was too hard to chew."

Gabby nodded.

"Without my magical treat, I can't make sure that bubble gum is chewy and

delicious," she said. "And it's not just me. With the Harvest Feast coming up, time is running out. If we don't find the three missing magical treats, the Harvest Feast at the Candy Factory will be ruined."

"Then there's no time to lose," said Kirsty. "We need to begin the search right away—and I think I know exactly where to start."

Goblin Gum

Kirsty turned to Rachel, bursting to explain her idea.

"Do you remember Olivia talking about the boys by the fence on the far side of the park?" she asked Rachel. "She said that they were blowing big bubbles with green bubble gum. But we couldn't even chew our gum, so why is

their gum making such perfect bubbles?
What if they are somehow using
Gabby's magic? I think they might be
goblins."

"Oh my goodness," said Gabby,
her eyes wide. "Do you really think
that my magical bubble gum could be
right here?"

"Let's find out," said Rachel.

She came out from under the slide and
peered across the park toward the fence.
Kirsty came to stand beside her.

"It's hard to tell," said Kirsty. "They
are all wearing hats, so we can't see if
they have green heads."

"Look at their hands," said Rachel.
"Goblins have pointy fingers, and that's
one thing they can't disguise."

Rachel and Kirsty exchanged a

knowing look. Their fingers were definitely pointy.

"They must be goblins," said Gabby, settling down on Rachel's shoulder. "But how can we get closer? They'll run off as soon as they see us."

"I've got an idea," said Rachel. "Gabby, can you disguise us as goblins? They won't run away if they think we're just like them. When we're close enough, we can put the plan into action. Goblins always like a competition, and we're going to give them one."

Gabby nodded, and the girls ducked back under the slide. She waved her wand, and a tickly feeling started in the girls' hands and spread all over their bodies. They watched each other, giggling as their skin turned green. Rachel saw Kirsty's nose bubble with warts and her ears grow larger. Kirsty giggled as Rachel's fingers grew pointy and her knees became knobby.

There was a final bright flash of light, and then Rachel and Kirsty were no longer girls. They were dressed in skinny jeans, T-shirts, and lime-green high-top sneakers. Under their hats, their heads were bald and bumpy.

"No one would guess that you're Kirsty Tate," said Rachel with a laugh. "I just hope that your aunt Helen doesn't come looking for us early."

Kirsty smiled, and held open her pocket so that Gabby could slip inside.

"Let's go," she said.

They headed across the park toward the fence. On the way they passed Olivia, who was still playing with the little girl they had seen earlier.

"Hi, Olivia," called Kirsty, forgetting for a moment that she didn't look like herself anymore.

Olivia looked a little confused, but waved to her.

"Whoops," said Kirsty, putting her hand over her mouth. "I have to remember that I'm in disguise."

The girls strolled over to the goblins, trying not to look too interested. The

goblins were still blowing bubbles.
Rachel waited until the bubble that the
tallest goblin was blowing went *POP*,
and then laughed.

"I can blow a bigger bubble than
that," she said in a boastful voice. "I can

blow a bigger bubble than anyone else here."

"Oh, no you can't," said the tallest goblin.

He started to blow another big bubble, and so did all the other goblins. Rachel and Kirsty watched as bubbles popped and splattered all over the goblins' faces.

"Kirsty, look," whispered Rachel.

She nodded her head in the direction of the bench. A goblin with droopy ears was sitting there, blowing a truly huge bubble. After the bubble burst, he held out his hand and squeezed his eyes shut, muttering something. Then a rectangle of green bubble gum appeared in his

hand. He popped it into his mouth and chewed it noisily. Then he started to blow an even bigger bubble than before.

"Goblins can't do their own magic," Kirsty whispered in Rachel's large green ear. "He must have Gabby's magical bubble gum!"

Code Pink Emergency

Rachel went over to where the droopy-eared goblin was sitting and bent down to talk to him.

"May I have some gum, please?" she asked politely. "I want to prove to everyone that I can blow the biggest bubbles."

The goblin looked at her in surprise.

"But of course," he said in a singsong voice. "How do you do, and please and thank you as well."

He lifted his hat and pulled out a huge, chewed-up wad of gum.

"Have some of this ABC gum," he said. "I've been keeping it especially for extra-polite goblins who mind their manners."

"What's ABC gum?" Rachel asked, surprised that he was being so nice.

"Already Been Chewed!" yelled the goblin, cackling with horrible laughter.

Rachel's heart sank.

"No, thanks," she said, and hurried quickly back to Kirsty.

"My idea didn't work," she said sadly. "I was too polite, and he laughed at me. Your turn, Kirsty."

"I've got a plan," said Kirsty. "I think! Wish me luck."

"Good luck," said Rachel, crossing her fingers and smiling at her friend.

Kirsty walked up to the goblin and

took a deep breath. Rachel had tried
being polite, and it hadn't worked. Kirsty
was going to have to be as rude as the
goblins were if she wanted to get the
magical gum back.

"Hey, you," she said in a squawky
voice. "Give me some fresh gum right
now, moldy breath. I want to blow a

giant bubble, and I want to do it now!"

The goblin scowled at her, but reached
one bony hand into his pocket and
pulled out pink, sparkling bubble gum.
A deliciously sweet
smell filled the air.
Immediately, Gabby
zoomed out of
Kirsty's pocket
and swooped
toward the
goblin's hand.

"Look out!"
shrieked a goblin
from behind Kirsty.
"It's a fairy!"

The droopy-eared goblin's bony fingers
closed around the gum. Then a large
lime-green sneaker stepped between

Rachel and Kirsty, and
bony elbows shoved
them aside. A goblin
with extra-big feet
blew a massive
bubble, and Gabby
could not get out
of the way quickly

enough. She was trapped in the bubble.

As Gabby tried to push her way out of the sticky bubble, the goblin roared with laughter. He stuck the bubble to the park fence and then scampered off toward the Candy Land factory, followed by all the other goblins.

"Quickly, we have to go after them," Gabby called out.

Rachel unstuck the bubble from the fence, and Kirsty poked her finger into it. With a loud *POP*, Gabby was free.

"Thank you for rescuing me," she said.

"It was horrible to feel trapped."

"Can you turn us into fairies?" Kirsty asked. "We'll be able to follow the goblins more quickly if we can fly."

Olivia and the little girl were not looking their way. Gabby waved her wand, and—*POP! POP!*—Rachel and Kirsty were goblins no longer. Now they were fluttering beside Gabby, their wings glimmering in the sunlight. They zoomed toward the factory side by side and slipped in through an open window.

The fairies were in a long hallway that had many doors. They looked both ways, but the hallway was empty.

"The goblins have disappeared," said Kirsty. "Where would they have gone?"

"We could split up and search for them," Gabby suggested.

"Wait," said Rachel suddenly. "There
are signs on these doors. Look—each one
leads to a different department."

They flew down the hallway, checking
each door sign.

"*Hard Candy Department*," Kirsty read out
loud. "*Gummy Candy Department. Chocolate*

Department. Marshmallow Department."

"*Bubble Gum Department!*" said Gabby with a squeak of excitement. "I bet they're in here."

The door was shut, but the gap

underneath it was big enough for a fairy to slip through.

Once they were inside, a man's heavy feet hurried toward them.

"Out of the way!" Rachel cried.

The fairies dived sideways and flew onto a high shelf. From there they could see that the Bubble Gum Department was in chaos. Workers in pink overalls were dashing left and right in a panic. An open door in the far corner of the room was labeled *Gum Testing*, and more workers were staggering out of it, their lips stuck together with

gum. A lady in a bubble-gum pink suit
was yelling into her phone.

"This is a Code Pink Emergency," she
cried. "The gum has turned extra sticky.

The gum testers are down.
I repeat, the gum testers
are down."

She listened for a
moment and then
put down the phone.
"Evacuate the
Bubble Gum
Department!" she
yelled to the other
workers. "Everyone
out!"

The workers
stampeded out of
the department, and
Rachel grabbed Kirsty
and Gabby by the hands.

"The goblins are behind
this," she said. "Come on, we have to go in."

Gabby squared her tiny fairy shoulders, and her wings fluttered. "Absolutely. We have to put a stop to this!"

"Things are about to get sticky," Kristy muttered. "Let's go in on the count of three. One, two, THREE!" she cried.

A Barrel of Gum

The fairies flew into the testing room. They saw little tables filled with brightly colored bubble gum, comfortable chairs, and plenty of whiteboards where testers could write notes about the gum. But there were no goblins.

"Over there," said Kirsty, spotting another open door.

The sign on the door said *Gum-Making Room.* As they flew toward it, Rachel spotted one of the Candy Land Helping Hands bags on a table. It was filled with bubble gum, and it had Olivia's name on it.

"Oh no," Rachel said with a groan. "Olivia's going to win a prize, but it won't be any good unless we can get the magical bubble gum back."

"Don't worry," said Kirsty in a

determined voice. "That's exactly what we're going to do."

They flew through the doorway into a noisy warehouse filled with clanking, hissing machines. A maze of conveyor belts circled the room. Some carried piles of unwrapped bubble gum and dumped them into chutes, which led to packaging machines. Others carried packs of bubble

gum to large Candy Land boxes.

The goblins were dancing on one of the conveyor belts, trampling on the gum. The droopy-eared goblin was throwing handfuls of bubble gum around like confetti. Another was kicking it into the air. They were cackling and squawking with the fun of mischief.

"We have to stop them," said Gabby with a groan. "They're going to ruin all the bubble gum unless I can get my magical treat back."

Suddenly, Kirsty noticed a big barrel of warm bubble gum mixture standing near one of the conveyor belts. The thick, sticky goo was waiting to be cooled and shaped.

"Gabby, I have an idea," she said. "Can you use your magic to move that barrel and reverse the conveyor belt?"

Gabby's eyes twinkled when she understood Kirsty's plan, and she nodded. Her wand flicked up and down like a conductor's baton, and then the barrel began to scrape across the floor. The bubble gum goo sloshed as the barrel bumped against the end of the conveyor belt. Then Gabby tapped her wand against the side of the conveyor belt, and it shuddered to a stop.

"What's wrong with it?" squawked the droopy-eared goblin. "Did it break?"

CLANK! The machinery went into reverse, and the conveyor belt sent the goblins whizzing back toward the barrel. One after another, they plopped into the pink mixture. They wriggled and jiggled, but it was no use. They were totally stuck in the gum.

"I can't move!" wailed the droopy-eared goblin.

"Get me out of here!" shouted another.

Rachel, Kirsty, and Gabby fluttered over to the barrel and perched on the rim.

"Gabby will get you out," said Kirsty, "but only after you return her magical bubble gum."

"No way," the goblins grumbled. "We're not doing anything you say, silly fairies."

They tried clambering over each other to get out, and they tried pushing each other out. Nothing worked. The fairies simply waited and watched. Eventually, the goblins started to whisper to each other. At first, some of them shook their heads, but eventually they were all nodding. Every single one of them looked miserable.

"Jack Frost is going to be so angry," the smallest goblin muttered. "I don't like it when he gets mad."

"Well, I don't like being stuck in a barrel," said the goblin with the droopy ears. "The fun's over."

He managed to squirm through the goo, and held his hand up in the air. He was holding Gabby's magic bubble gum.

A smile lit up Gabby's face as she took

the bubble gum
in her delicate
fingers. It shrank
to fairy size at
once. Then she
waved her wand
and spoke the
words of a spell.

*"Return these
goblins to the floor.
They won't cause
trouble anymore.
Clean them up and give
them gum,
To keep them all from feeling glum."*
Suddenly, the goblins found themselves
standing beside the barrel, as clean as
they were before they fell in. Each of
them was holding bubble gum. Big grins

started to spread
across all of their
faces.

"Come on,
let's go
back to the
playground,"
said the goblin
with the droopy
ears. "I'm
going to blow
the biggest
bubble ever."

"No way,"
the smallest
goblin retorted.
"Your bubble
will look like a
tiny, wrinkly raisin

compared to mine. I'm the best, and my bubble will be, too. Just you wait!"

Squabbling loudly, the goblins ran out of the room, pushing and shoving each other to try to get through the door first.

Kirsty and Rachel smiled at each other, relieved. Putting the goblins into a sticky situation had worked!

Big Bubbles

Gabby waved her wand again, and immediately the room was sparkling clean. In fact, it looked better than it had before. The barrel was back in its original place, and the bubble gum was traveling neatly along the conveyor belts. There was no sign that the goblins had ever been there.

Gabby hugged Rachel and Kirsty, and

then gently tapped their shoulders with her wand. They returned to their normal size in the blink of an eye.

Just then, they heard a sound that grew

louder and louder.

"It's footsteps," said Rachel in alarm.
"Someone's coming."

Gabby slipped into Rachel's pocket

just as the factory workers came back
into the room, following the lady in the
pink suit. Everyone looked a lot happier.

"I'm so happy that all the gum testers'
mouths have been unstuck," the lady
said. "Everything seems to be back to

normal in here, so please return to your work."

Pressing themselves back against the wall, Rachel and Kirsty edged around the room and out the door. They had just reached the Helping Hands bag of bubble gum when they heard a familiar voice.

"Girls? What a surprise to see you in here!"

It was Aunt Helen. She came over to them, smiling.

"I see you've found the next Helping Hands prize," she said. "The winner is a girl named Olivia, who has been a wonderful playground buddy on our Candy Land playground. Would you like to come and present the prize with me right now?"

The girls agreed eagerly, relieved that Aunt Helen hadn't asked them to explain what they were doing in the Bubble Gum Department. Soon they were heading toward the playground. More children had arrived, and the goblins were there, too. Aunt Helen called Olivia over to her, and everyone gathered around.

"Olivia, the other children who use this playground think that you are a very kind person," said Aunt Helen. "They have voted for you to be the winner of today's Helping Hands award. Congratulations! We hope that you enjoy your prize."

Olivia's eyes filled with surprised, happy tears as Rachel and Kirsty gave her the bag of bubble gum. Everyone burst into applause.

"Thank you, all," Olivia said, gazing around at the friendly, smiling faces. "I hope you'll share it with me."

She passed around the bubble gum, and soon everyone was blowing big, beautiful bubbles—even Aunt Helen!

"This gum is deliciously soft and
chewy," said Kirsty. "I'm so happy."

"The goblins are happy, too," said
Rachel with a smile.

The goblins were joining in with the
bubble-blowing, and even clapped when

Olivia managed to blow the biggest
bubble of all. While everyone else was
laughing and playing, Rachel and Kirsty
ducked under the slide. Gabby fluttered

out of Rachel's pocket and gave each of
them a gentle kiss on the cheek.

"Thank you for helping me today," she
said. "We are one step closer to making
the Harvest Feast a success."

"Please tell Franny
and Shelley that
we'll be ready
to help find the
other missing
treats," Kirsty
said, looking
determined.

Gabby blew
a fairy-size
bubble. Its
color changed
and shimmered
from pink to
lilac to purple
and back to pink
again. It was the
tiniest, most perfect
bubble that the girls

had ever seen. As they stared at it, Gabby disappeared with a *POP*. She had gone back to Fairyland, but her bubble drifted upward, higher and higher into the sky.

"Do you think that we'll be able to find the other two magical objects for the Sweet Fairies before the Harvest Feast?" Kirsty asked her best friend.

Rachel nodded.

"Definitely. We won't let Jack Frost ruin things for the fairies," she said. "But right now, I want to go down this amazing slide again. Race you!"

RAINBOW magic
THE SWEET FAIRIES

Rachel and Kirsty have found Monica
and Gabby's missing magical items.
Now it's time for them to help

Franny
the Jelly Bean Fairy!

Join their next adventure in this
special sneak peek . . .

Surprises

"This is a bumpy ride!" said Kirsty Tate with a laugh.

She and her best friend, Rachel Walker, giggled as they bounced up and down. Kirsty's aunt Helen patted the dashboard.

"I love this good old Candy Land van," she said. "Even if it is a little noisy and bumpy sometimes."

Candy Land was the candy factory just outside Wetherbury Village, and Aunt Helen was lucky enough to work there.

"Candy Land is my second favorite thing about Wetherbury," said Rachel.

"What's your favorite?" asked Kirsty.

"Staying with you, of course," said Rachel with a grin. "It's always magical."

Rachel had come to visit Kirsty over the school break. Ever since they had become best friends, they had also been good friends with the fairies. Magic always seemed to follow them around when they were together. Sometimes they thought that it was as if their friendship cast a very special spell.

This time, Monica the Marshmallow Fairy had whisked them away to the Fairyland Candy Factory, where candy grew on trees. They had met the other Sweet Fairies, who used their magical objects to make sure that all candy was sweet and delicious. The fairies were getting ready for the annual Harvest Feast, and asked Rachel and Kirsty if they would like to come. But then Jack Frost had appeared with his goblins. He had stolen the Sweet Fairies' magical objects so that he could keep all candy for himself.

Kirsty and Rachel had helped two of the Sweet Fairies get their magical objects back, but there were still two more to find. However, today they had something else on their minds. They were on their way to see a boy named Tal, who volunteered as a dog walker at the Wetherbury Animal Shelter.

"I can't wait to see Tal's face when he finds out that he's a winner," said Kirsty.

RAINBOW magic

Which Magical Fairies Have You Met?

- ❑ The Rainbow Fairies
- ❑ The Weather Fairies
- ❑ The Jewel Fairies
- ❑ The Pet Fairies
- ❑ The Sports Fairies
- ❑ The Ocean Fairies
- ❑ The Princess Fairies
- ❑ The Superstar Fairies
- ❑ The Fashion Fairies
- ❑ The Sugar & Spice Fairies
- ❑ The Earth Fairies
- ❑ The Magical Crafts Fairies
- ❑ The Baby Animal Rescue Fairies
- ❑ The Fairy Tale Fairies
- ❑ The School Day Fairies
- ❑ The Storybook Fairies
- ❑ The Friendship Fairies

SCHOLASTIC

HiT entertainment

Find all of your favorite fairy friends at
scholastic.com/rainbowmagic

RMFAIRY17

RAINBOW magic™

Which Magical Fairies Have You Met?

- ❏ Joy the Summer Vacation Fairy
- ❏ Holly the Christmas Fairy
- ❏ Kylie the Carnival Fairy
- ❏ Stella the Star Fairy
- ❏ Shannon the Ocean Fairy
- ❏ Trixie the Halloween Fairy
- ❏ Gabriella the Snow Kingdom Fairy
- ❏ Juliet the Valentine Fairy
- ❏ Mia the Bridesmaid Fairy
- ❏ Flora the Dress-Up Fairy
- ❏ Paige the Christmas Play Fairy
- ❏ Emma the Easter Fairy
- ❏ Cara the Camp Fairy
- ❏ Destiny the Rock Star Fairy
- ❏ Belle the Birthday Fairy
- ❏ Olympia the Games Fairy
- ❏ Selena the Sleepover Fairy

- ❏ Cheryl the Christmas Tree Fairy
- ❏ Florence the Friendship Fairy
- ❏ Lindsay the Luck Fairy
- ❏ Brianna the Tooth Fairy
- ❏ Autumn the Falling Leaves Fairy
- ❏ Keira the Movie Star Fairy
- ❏ Addison the April Fool's Day Fairy
- ❏ Bailey the Babysitter Fairy
- ❏ Natalie the Christmas Stocking Fairy
- ❏ Lila and Myla the Twins Fairies
- ❏ Chelsea the Congratulations Fairy
- ❏ Carly the School Fairy
- ❏ Angelica the Angel Fairy
- ❏ Blossom the Flower Girl Fairy
- ❏ Skyler the Fireworks Fairy
- ❏ Giselle the Christmas Ballet Fairy
- ❏ Alicia the Snow Queen Fairy

31901063796181

SCHOLASTIC

Find all of your favorite fairy friends at
scholastic.com/rainbowmagic

3 stories in each one!

HIT entertainment

RMSPECIA